Thank you for purchasing my e-book.

Please leave a review voluntarily.

About the book

BODY IN THE WAVES

Natalija was raped ten years ago and did not tell anyone who did it. When she goes on a vacation to the Adriatic Sea, the Island of Pag, her rapist, Denis, shows up, as the boyfriend of her future sister-in-law. He was not punished for his act because Natalija was afraid of moral judgment. Denis changes his behavior toward Natalija, but his intentions are not pure.

About the author

My first name is Kristina. I am using the pseudonym Gallo as my alias in writing.

I live in Croatia. I was always rebellious, which comes to life in my books. English is not my native language. I was blogging and writing columns for internet magazines.

I became an indie author in 2017 when I published my first book on Amazon. My love for adrenaline and thriller movies inspired me, and I found myself in dark suspense and mysterious novels.

Enjoy reading, and I would appreciate a review.

BODY IN THE WAVES

KRISTINA GALLO

Thriller suspense

Natalija was angry. She imagined Maja, a twenty-five-year-old brunette, with her new boyfriend. She was a promiscuous and shallow girl, her favorite things being fashion magazines and a suitable outfit. She always found something interesting to say about whatever Natalija wore.

She would borrow stuff from Natalija, like purses or lipstick. Natalija was a designer, so it was a kind of compliment to her, but she did not like Maja's approach. The girl was pushy. At first, she had acted like she was Natalija's best friend, but Natalija did not want to get close with her.

After Maja had returned a purse in a critical condition, burned from a cigarette, she told her it was the last time she would loan her anything.

Bruno came with a few paper bags full of groceries.

"Do you think I should cook?" Natalija asked with a smirk. She had no intention to cook for Maja, or anyone else. She was on summer vacation, and this place has excellent restaurants. Besides, she had not expected guests.

"No, I will make some hamburgers. I bought a pastry and some meat. I will bake it fast. There are beers too." Bruno was always giving. It was his weakness, his inability to say no. Natalija did not pity him. He invited his guests, so he could take care of them. She made another vodka with juice for herself and went to the terrace.

After half an hour, she saw a car near their apartment. It was a red Audi, and two people stepped out of it.

Maja was in her usual: a sexy outfit. With her short skirt, big summer hat, and high heels, she looked like she had just come from fashion week. It bothered Natalija so much that Maja was such an attention whore and did not hide it.

The guy beside Maja was tall and blond with a muscular body, but Natalija could not see his face well. His black sunglasses hid his eyes. He was dressed like some kind of rapper, his trousers baggy and with holes, intentionally made to complete a rebellious look.

Natalija got up from her chair. Something was upsetting her. The guy reminded her of someone she knew who liked a similar Kanye West style, someone she forgot years ago.

When they arrived at the door, Natalija saw a familiar face.

"No, it can't be true," she murmured, her hands shaking.

"Hi, pals." Maja's influential voice broke the silence. "How are you? Ready for the party? Let me introduce you to my boyfriend, Denis."

The blond guy took off his shades and approached Bruno, shook his hand, and spread his palm to catch Natalija's hand. When he spoke, she had no doubt he was the guy from her nightmare.

"I am Denis. Nice to meet you." He spoke politely, as expected from someone who was a guest.

Natalija's glass fell on the floor. Her vodka with juice made a yellow puddle, and pieces of glass shattered around. She apologized with a trembling voice. "I am sorry, I must clean this."

She vanished into the kitchen looking for a broom, while the gazes of her guests followed her walk. They looked at her curiously.

"I think she did not sleep well." Bruno tried to calm the situation, wondering what was going on with his fiancée.

...

Natalija locked the door. She did not want to see anyone. She recalled her dark memories, and male voices mixed up in her mind. Broken sentences were jumbled in her brain, words like "slut," "whore," and "bimbo" buzzed in her ears like an alarm.

Denis's face smirked when she rejected his handshake. She was sure he remembered who she was, but he played his role of hide-and-seek masterfully.

Chapter 2

10 years ago, summer vacation

Crikvenica, a city by the Adriatic Sea, Croatia

A white Porsche was driving fast along the curves. It got near the edge of the road, and the ledge led straight to the abyss. Crazy driving was a source of adrenaline for the three drunk guys in the car.

The driver, Denis, was giggling like a lunatic, and his front passenger, Andrej, told him to carefully swap places and suggested taking over the car.

"Don't be silly, pussy. I can drive normally. Don't cry like a granny. I only drank one beer. The police wouldn't even care," Denis said and pulled the brake.

The car spun in a circle, and the girl in the back seat screamed. She was blonde, had a slim physique, and was dressed in a long summer skirt that was now torn because of the material stashed between the seats.

"Don't cry, honey. We will not die." Luka, the guy beside her, laughed like a clown and took a sip from his beer. He was not loud like his friends. He just wanted to fit in the circle.

Denis somehow avoided the car heading toward him and finally stopped near the road. He saw a restaurant and took a break.

People in the restaurant peered with interest at the small group, three guys and a lovely girl in her twenties. Her hair was flying in the wind like a flag, and her torn skirt looked like it came from a scarecrow's outfit. The blonde girl noticed their curious gazes and made a knot from the torn parts of her skirt.

"Natalija, you made a new fashion statement?" Denis asked her and gave her a thumbs-up. "I love to see your legs. Show it, honey. You have nothing to be ashamed of."

"I ruined it. It was a new dress." Natalija sighed. "Now I look like a tramp."

"Oh, come on, relax and have a drink. You will buy another one when we get back. Now, we need to go to the beach and swim. This fucking drive made me nervous. I need to relax in the sea. I'm sweating like a pig."

They sat at a table in the corner, and the server told Andrej he had to put on his shirt. His torso was naked, and his shirt was around his waist, like a rag. Andrej dressed, swearing and flipping his middle finger at the server.

Luka sat quietly in the corner. He had not said a word since they walked through the door. He just looked at Natalija curiously. He did not know her well. What was a girl like her doing keeping the company of hooligans? Andrej and Denis had each spent a few months in jail, because of an accident they had caused, but it did not stop local girls from fighting for their attention.

Andrej had ruined his previous car, and Denis had been driving drunk and faster than the speed limit. They had wounded a guy with a bike, who stayed alive only with the help of destiny. Now, they must have had luck again. This Porsche could slide off and into the abyss, but some kind of influential force had stopped the disaster.

They had met Natalija in the nightclub and drank together. She liked Denis; everyone knew it. He was a playboy and women adored him, so Natalija was not an exception. They talked and joked, and after a few drinks, he suggested that she come with them to the seaside, introducing his idea like a great adventure.

Natalija had known Denis since high school, and she was secretly in love with him. She was not afraid to accept his offer because she knew his friends too, and it was an opportunity to get close to him.

"I don't like it. It is cold. I want to get out of here." Natalija stood and walked across the rocky bottom, but then she yelled.

"Are you stupid? Don't you see there are sea urchins everywhere?" Denis laughed, and it echoed down the coast.

Natalija slipped on a rock and fell into the sea. She was in shallow water but tried to swim over the rocks to get to the beach. She stood on a sea urchin, and thorns get stuck in her foot.

Suddenly, she felt Denis's arms around her waist.

"Take it easy. Let's get out, and I will see if I can help you with it." Denis carried her in his arms.

She sat on her towel feeling helpless while he took her feet in his lap. His eyes watched her carefully. In his eyes was a look of hunger and greed. Denis felt his penis get hard, and he kissed Natalija.

"What are you doing?" she asked and tried to move away from his embrace.

"Don't you like me, honey? Everyone talks, so I know you want me. You have been following me around for months." Denis smiled confidently. He was used to dealing with girls who chased him.

"I don't follow you, Denis. I like you, but you can't throw me in the water like a toy." Natalija moved his hand from her breasts.

"Oh, why are you acting like an innocent virgin now? I heard stories about you. They say you are very hot." Denis approached her carefully, then grabbed her hair. He pulled her closer and pushed her onto the towel.

"Please leave me alone. You misunderstood me." Natalija stuttered and moved her leg.

She kicked him in the stomach, and the color of Denis's face changed.

"Are you playing with me, bitch? Why did you come with us in my car? You wanted to fuck with all of us, didn't you?"

Natalija tried to make her voice calmer, while Denis held her neck. "I was drunk when you picked me up. I was not thinking clearly. Just let me go. I am sorry, I should not have come here with you."

"Okay, I will let you go. But first, kiss me." He stared at her like a beast.

Natalija nodded and gave him a kiss with her lips squeezed together.

"You call that a kiss? Give me a proper kiss, honey. I am not your brother."

Denis pulled her and pushed his tongue into her mouth. His fingers inserted into her vagina. Natalija slapped him, but Denis returned her slap with his fist to her mouth, so her hair fell over her face.

"You want it rough, little bitch? I will show you now." He lay on top of her with all his weight. He was five foot eleven and just shy of two hundred pounds, so his body was a burden on a girl of only 110 pounds and barely over five feet tall.

Besides, he trained at the gym every week. His muscles were firm and his arms were strong, like steel. He spread her legs while she was half-conscious.

"Now, what do we have here, little pussy? Let me see." Denis smiled like an animal and put his fist inside her vagina.

Tears ran down Natalija's face. She tried to bite him, but he slapped her harder. He turned to look around himself. The beach was empty, with no nosey people around. Only seagulls flew over them, asking for food. Nothing could stop him now.

He threw his wet pants to the side and entered Natalija.

"Oh yes, you are so tight, honey. I like it so much," he repeated, while he moved inside her and squeezed her nipples with his fingertips. She lay on the towel, stiff like a doll, while blood dripped from her lips.

Denis moaned with pleasure. He held her palm over her mouth to prevent her from screaming. When he was done, he pulled out and sprayed his semen across her belly. Then he grabbed his pants and stood.

"I am not driving you back, little bitch. You need to learn your lesson. No girl will cross Denis. Understand?" He wiped his hands, sticky from semen, on the towel where she was lying like a corpse.

The first thing Natalija remembered when she opened her eyes was the sound of seagulls above the beach, like birds mocking her. She was a discarded thing on the beach, used for Denis's desires.

Her hair was wet and messy from the saltwater, and a white, sticky track of Denis's semen had spread, looking like a mark. It labeled her.

She washed in the cold sea, and the pain between her legs was strong like someone had tickled her with the edge of a knife. The sea salt bit her wounds, and her lips were swollen. The pain of humiliation was bigger; she felt like a worthless rag.

Then she heard slow steps behind her. The shadow of a man approached her, and he sat near her on the sand.

Chapter 3

The nightmare returns

Bruno persistently tapped on the door until Natalija opened it. Her room was dark, so Bruno opened the curtains. He had never seen Natalija in such a condition, so he was worried. She was sitting on the bed and staring ahead as if she were meditating.

"What happened to you, dear? Is it from the weed I gave you two hours ago? You smoked too much, didn't you?"

"Did they leave? "Natalija murmured through her teeth.

"What is the problem with my sister? I know you don't like each other but show some manners and at least play nice."

"Please leave me alone. I don't feel well. She is not the center of the world, so get out of here." Natalija had no patience to explain, and her voice was raised to the level of screaming.

Bruno left the room. Denis and Maja were waiting in the foyer.

He told them in an apologetic tone, "She doesn't feel well; she ate a hamburger this morning and is nauseated now. I am sorry."

Denis and Maja looked at each other and said, almost in unison.

"We are going home to unpack our things. We just arrived. See you at the party?"

"Yes, of course." Bruno nodded. He was so distracted, he did not even notice when they left the room.

.....

Memories, the year 2007

The wind was blowing, and Natalija's skin was chilled. She turned her wet face toward the guy next to her. It was Luka, who looked at her curiously. Her nose was bleeding, and the blood mixed with her tears.

"What happened here, Natalija? Denis kicked me out of the car because I did not want to give him my money for gas. So it seems I will return on a bus. We will go together, right?"

Natalija stuttered. "Nothing. We just argued."

Luka came closer to her. "Your lips are broken. And you have a scratch on your neck."

Natalija trembled. The tone in her voice changed.

"He pushed me... and I slapped him, so he—"

"Oh my God. You had sex? He was bragging about how you got what you asked for. I mean, he is a jerk, and I am sure you did not ask him for anything."

"He raped me," Natalija whispered and looked down at the sand on her feet.

Luka's face darkened. He squeezed his fists. "If you are going to report him, I will support you."

"Thanks, but I will not report him. I don't want to go to the police; I don't want to go to court either. The last thing I need is to recall this all over again."

"You will let him go free as nothing happened?"

"His family is rich. He can afford the best lawyers. What are my chances? I was with three guys without panties, drunk, and I accepted to go with him alone."

"You have bruises. At least you should go to the doctor to get checked out."

"No, I don't want to. Just let's go together to the bus. I want to go home."Luka gave her a hand to get up. He did not agree with her decision, but he was always a gentleman, and he stood beside her. At the very least, he did not want to upset her or for her to run off alone; he wanted Natalija to feel safe.

Present time, 2017

In the afternoon, Natalija made coffee and went to the terrace with two cups. Bruno did not want to upset her, so he sat in front of her, expecting her to talk about her feelings.

He put two tickets on the table, trying to cheer her up.

"Are we going to the party tonight? Skrillex is coming to the Noa Beach club. Remember we made plans to go?"

"Sure. I need to see what I will wear." Natalija's mood had changed. It seemed like nothing weird had happened.

"Are you feeling okay? I am worried about you."

"I am okay. Maybe the weed was the problem. I smoked too much and mixed it with vodka and juice. It was a poor combination; I blacked out."

Bruno did not look persuaded. Something was strange in her behavior, and he wanted to look further into what was going on. Natalija would never miss the opportunity to argue with

Maja, and it was not Natalija's style to hide in a room like a frightened child. Also, Natalija could handle a few joints. They smoked together from time to time, so the bad trip could not be a reason for her weird behavior.

....

Meanwhile, Maja and Denis went to the hotel room to unpack their things. While Maja was showering, Denis smoked a cigarette, and his memory passed through his mind like it were yesterday.

Zagreb, Zrinjevac Park, 2007

He met Natalija in the Zrinjevac Park a week after the event. She was rushing with a coffee in her hand, and he jumped in front of her. She spilled half of the coffee on her feet and trembled with fear.

"What do you want?" Her eyes widened. She wanted to continue her walk, but he stopped her, catching her free hand.

"Don't be afraid of me. I want to talk to you." He pulled her onto a nearby bench, trying to calm her down.

"I don't want to talk to you. I will scream, you piece of shit."

"Just give me five minutes," Denis said in a calm voice.

Natalija stared at him, wiping her feet with a napkin.

Denis pulled out his wallet and showed her a Euro banknote. Then he pulled out another one. In completion, he offered her five hundred Euros.

"Please accept my apology. I was drunk and high. I did not want to hurt you. Thanks for not reporting me. I want you to take this."

Natalija laughed uncontrollably. "You are a bigger idiot than I thought, Denis. Do you think you can pay for my dignity? You can wipe your ass with that. Just leave me alone, get out of here. Don't approach me ever again, or I will hurt you."

Natalija opened her purse and pulled out her pepper spray. She pressed the button, and Denis coughed.

He saw her leaving through the thick, white fog.

***

It was the last time he'd had any contact with her. Ten years later, he saw her again. She was prettier than he remembered.

Her breasts were bigger because she had put on some weight, and her curves were visible. Did she remember him? Based on her reaction, he supposed she did.

....

Present time

Maja interrupted his reveries. She stood in front of him. "Are you here, or is your head in the clouds? I asked you if you had our tickets for the party.

Denis opened his eyes and looked at her like he had just woken up from a nightmare. "Yes, of course. The tickets are in my wallet."

"Did you watch the weather forecast today? The wind is blowing like crazy; they said a hundred twenty kilometers per hour." Maja's brow wrinkled. "It is an open-air party. If I wear a short skirt... No, I will stay in pants."

The Island of Pag was known for its strong winds, called bura in Croatian. Last week, tourists could not get out of their rooms because of the wind's strength. It was impossible to swim on the beach because the wind made the sea cold, and it was carrying branches and trash around.

Old trees were broken and ruined, and the wind speed was a threat to the cars parked around. It could cause damage. Chris Brown was supposed to have had a concert in Zrće Beach, but he canceled it because of the bura. He was there for ten minutes and left. He was afraid the wooden platform would break under the crowd and it was not safe.

The club was situated outdoors on a huge platform above the sea, with two floors, a VIP area, a beach, and main stage area, a lounge zone, a yacht club, pools, and a few nets above the sea.

"What will I wear?" Natalija asked Denis, turning around in front of her mirror.

"The red dress that fits you well. It is long enough and practical. Think about the wind outside," Bruno said.

"You are right. I need a jacket too. Are we going on foot?"

It was typical for them to go on foot along the road because Bruno liked to drink, so he did not want to go by car. Police were everywhere, and he did not want to cross them while drunk. Also, he and Natalija were drinking together, which made their walking funnier and saved them money, because beverages at the club were expensive.

"I will prepare you a vodka and lemon." Bruno winked. He was happy because Natalija's mood was good again. Maybe it had been the weed. Next time, he would watch out how many joints she smoked.

Chapter 4

The party

The clouds changed color, from white to gray. It looked like a fluffy ball made itself dirty, and the entire sky was playing the game. The wind was wild, blowing fast and carrying abandoned empty bottles.

Natalija and Bruno walked near the road, holding a flashlight because some streetlamps did not produce light. They carefully watched the cars driving around because where they were was not recommended for pedestrians.

"I am freezing," Natalija said, then sipped her vodka and orange juice they had put in a bigger bottle.

"Drink it, you will get warm," Bruno said and lit his cigarette. It was a real challenge because the wind was blowing like crazy, so he held his lighter and covered it with his other hand. "I should call Maja to pick us up with their car."

"No chance. I don't like the guy who is with her." Finally, Natalija said it. She held her burden, but she could say at least something, even if it was not the whole truth.

"He looks like a prick. That is true. But how can you hate someone you just met?"

"It is not hate. I just don't like her boyfriends. She always picks guys with big egos and then she complains they broke her heart," Natalija said, trying to sound cool.

Somewhere in the background, the sound of thunder broke Bruno's silence. "A storm is coming," he said thoughtfully. "I wonder how the party will go."

In front of Noa beach club's stage was an enormous crowd. Many young people were there to see Skrillex, a talented DJ who was the main guest. It was 11:00 p.m., and he was set to perform at midnight.

Over in the corner of the crowd, near the toilets, Bruno saw his sister with Denis. They were drinking cocktails and waved at them.

"I will wait for you here," Natalija said. "You will find me near the dance floor."

"Okay, I will not be long, only enough to say hello to them."

Natalija bought a White Russian to increase the effect of her vodka. She was dancing in place, but the electronic music made her step faster. She did not see Maja as she approached her.

"That drink is too sugary. You will puke," Maja said in her ear, and Natalija moved a step back.

"What do you want from me?"

"I came here to talk. The men are talking, so I will talk to you, Natalija. You always think you are better than me. I think you are jealous." Maja raised her voice to talk over the loud music.

"I want you to leave me alone. Go to your boyfriend-rapist," Natalija snapped and finished her drink.

"What are you saying? Are you drunk already? What do you know about my Denis?"

"Ask him what he did ten years ago on the beach, how he spent his vacation. I am sure he has an interesting story to tell."

"You are out of your mind. Stupid bitch." Maja took her glass and spilled the drink over Natalija's head.

At that moment, the wind was fierce, and boards on the platform creaked. Heavy rain fell, but the music was still playing.

"The hell... What is this? "Natalija yelled and peered around, looking for her boyfriend.

She saw only the crowd as they ran toward the exit in panic. Boards fell from the wooden ceiling and smashed glasses to the ground. Servers were running around, collecting the broken pieces.

She went to the bar to find shelter. Waves from the sea were bigger and faster and splashing the space. Even the toilets were probably already full of water. She felt like she was on the Titanic; the club was rocking, and the wind was making a mess. She desperately needed to pee, but she was afraid of using a toilet.

Her bladder was full. Natalija supposed nobody will notice her, so she peed in her pants. Her urine would mix with her wet clothes, so the smell would vanish.

She saw Bruno waving at her from the other side.

"Get out of here, lady!" the server yelled at her. "You can get injured. It is not safe."

Natalija moved closer to the iron fence outside, but she slipped on the wet floor. Two guys, dancing in a drunken stupor next to her, did not notice her and pushed her unintentionally. She lost her balance and fell into the sea.

It was dark, and the water was cold. Her dress wrapped around her body and made her body heavier. Waves splashed against her while she tried to swim along the surface to reach the coast. Her heart was throbbing, and she was having a hard time catching her breath.

Suddenly she felt arms around her. Someone was dragging her. She did not see the person in the dark. She swallowed saltwater and spat it.

"Don't be afraid. We are here, just hold on." She heard Denis's deep voice. He must have been the one gripping her.

Bruno was on the shore with a jacket. He covered her and said thanks to Denis, looking at him curiously.

"Just wait here. I will pick you up." Denis ran through the parking lot, dragging Natalija to his car.

"You should take off your clothes," Denis said with concern. "Just try to get dry. You will find my beach towel on the back seat. We will stay here for a while. It should calm down. I have a notification on my phone about the weather forecast."

"Damn it." Natalija was coughing and did not even say thanks. She entered the car, took off her clothes, and wrapped herself in a towel she found in the back seat. She was sneezing and trembling, but she stayed quiet. She opened the car door and waved at Bruno, to notify him she was okay.

Maja looked at them from a distance with disbelief, her brow furrowed.

She grabbed her brother Bruno under his arm and said, "They know each other from before? She said some weird things earlier."

"I don't know. I will talk to her when she calms down. Something in her story doesn't seem right."

Bruno had many doubts, and he did not miss Denis's eyes on Natalija's breasts when he was carrying her from the water. He looked at her with lust. It was not a glare of someone who had saved her life; it was a hunter's. Denis behaved like he had caught his prey.

The storm stopped, but Bruno did not intend to stay at the party. He accepted Denis's invitation to jump in the car, and they traveled together in silence, avoiding a discussion about anything.

Chapter 5

Two days later

It was a full moon. Natalija struggled to sleep. The moonlight had an insomnia effect, compounded by the events that had happened earlier. She saw Denis's human side and started questioning her feelings. What he had done in the past was unforgivable, but if she did not react properly then, why should she hold a grudge now?

There was a lot of bitterness inside of her, but with the events from the other night, something different grew within her, a seed of tenderness mixed with gratitude. Maybe it was Denis's compensation attempt for what he had done in the past, but he surprised her by jumping into the sea to save her. Had she developed Stockholm syndrome after ten years of inner pain and shame?

She was smoking on the terrace when Bruno approached her from behind. "I think it is time we talked, and I want the whole truth."

"What do you mean?"

"It is obvious you are hiding something from me. I feel like a stranger, and I don't like it. What happened between you and Denis?"

"Is this a police interrogation?" Natalija frowned. "I don't want to talk about this. It is the past. It can't change."

Bruno let out a sigh. "Fine, I suppose I am not someone you should confide in."

"Don't misunderstand me. I don't feel good about this issue. I am going for a walk. I need air." Natalija threw her cigarette butt over the balcony.

It upset her. She never had handled the pressure well, and Bruno was insisting to dig inside her soul, about things she did not want to remember.

....

The sound of water and singing filled the bathroom. Denis was showering, and it was his habit to sing Bon Jovi's "Livin' on a Prayer." Maja could not stand it, but she did not complain because of his short temper. Once she had nagged him about how he never bought her things like boyfriends did.

His reaction was to yell at her like a lunatic. He never hit her, but there were a few times when she had given in to their arguments because something in his voice frightened her. She did not want to see where his boundaries were.

She did not know much about him. They met six months ago at a party. He was ten years older than her but was not mature for his age. He was thirty, and his behavior was sometimes childish, like a hooligan with no rules. She knew he'd had many girlfriends, but it did not bother her too much. He was a handsome guy, so it was normal he caught the interest of many women.

A week ago, her opinion changed. For the first time, she felt jealousy. It was a woman's intuition. She noticed how Denis peered at Natalija the first day they met. After Natalija had said strange things in the club, Maja wanted to know more, but she did not dare to ask her boyfriend any details.

While he was showering, she used the opportunity to dig into his phone. She looked at albums of photos and smiled at first because a photo of herself in a swimsuit was the first thing she saw.

Then she noticed a folder named Princess and opened it. Natalija's photos were in that album, shocking Maja. The photos had been taken from Natalija's Facebook and other social media where she had posted it. Denis had saved it, which did not comfort Maja. It made her furious.

It looked like Denis was obsessed with Natalija.

Or he knew her, and she meant something to him? One was a photo taken from behind. Denis must have taken the shot on the beach when Natalija did not know he was there. It was freaky.

"Damn idiot." Maja was swearing, and suddenly, the bathroom door opened. The phone fell from her hands to the floor, and the screen broke.

Denis's jaw dropped from an unpleasant surprise. "Are you crazy? What are you doing with my phone?"

"I am sorry. I will buy you a new one if the phone doesn't work," Maja murmured while he tried to turn the phone on. Luckily, it was only the glass on the display that had cracked. The signal was still there.

"How do you dare touch my phone? Did I permit you to do this?" Denis raised his voice. He stood with his arms crossed but looked like he was ready to hit her.

"Why do you have Natalija's photos in your album? I can tell my brother about this."

"Listen, stupid woman. Are you trying to control me? If you dare to talk about this with your fucking brother, you will regret it. Stay away from my things, and get out from my sight!" Denis yelled, and Maja left the room.

....

The air at night was fresh, so Natalija took a deep breath. It soothed her. Bruno respected her wish to be alone, but he followed her from a distance, concerned about her actions.

She sat on a bench near the beach and peered at the sea. It was mystical at night. The beach was rocky and waves splashed the cliffs. Somewhere in the distance were small boats, sailing peacefully while the moonlight spread its glow.

A motorboat sat near the beach, and the tall man next to it caught the buoy tied to the concrete, to set up the motorboat. He had a flashlight, and the light revealed his face. It was Denis. Natalija was wondering what he was doing there in the middle of the night. He noticed her and waved.

"How are you today? Are you feeling well?"

"I am fine, thank you. But isn't it late to sail?"

"I love night activities." Denis giggled. "I was checking how the new motor is working. This beast is good. What are you doing here alone? Where is your boyfriend?"

"I have insomnia, so I took a walk."

Denis sat next to her, and their knees almost touched. He wrapped her in his arms. "If you want to talk about anything, I am listening."

Natalija did not move his arm. She was silent and then she cried. Tears streamed down her face. She could not stop herself.

Denis took her in an embrace, trying to make her calm. "I can't fix what I have done, but I can promise to take care of you."

Natalija wiped her tears and looked at his eyes. The moon shone through his blue eyes, and she longed to kiss him. Denis had an instinct and guessed her wishes, so he kissed her softly and then moved to a distance.

"I must go. I don't want to cause you trouble," he said and walked away with a satisfied smile on his face. His plan was working. It was only a matter of time before he would succeed.

He took out his phone when he was a safe distance away and called the number. "She will be ready in a few days. You can pack your luggage and come here. I reserved a house near the beach for you."

The deep male voice on the other line said, "I admire how you set up this thing so fast. You must give me the recipe for how you do it."

...

Bruno sped up his steps. He heard a part of the conversation between Denis and his friend on the phone, but he could not connect the meaning. He was sure of one thing. Natalija was in a dangerous predicament. She was in trouble, but Bruno did not know what kind of trouble it was. He had to find out before it was too late.

Chapter 6

The plan from hell

The house by the sea got a new purpose. Andrej wanted to make a movie studio. In the corner were cameras and chairs. A red curtain created a movie-like atmosphere, and a computer was on the desk, with open internet tabs.

Three half-naked girls walked by in high heels, carrying cocktails on their plates. Two men were drinking and laughing at their jokes, smoking cigarettes, and slapping women on their butts.

Andrej wanted to make a movie for adults. He had done a few amateur movies and posted them in Gonzo, but with so much competition, many people did not notice that movie. Nowadays, people easily got bored, and a naked body was not a special thing. Even threesomes did not help.

He also had technical problems. The HD camera was making misty images, and the principal actors looked like shadows.

Like his friend Bruno, Andrej was a spoiled son, educated by rich parents. They had a few bakeries in his city, but he did not want to work for anyone, anywhere.

Andrej tried to get into the Academy for Drama and Art to earn a diploma as a movie director, but he didn't. He worked some temporary jobs and then borrowed money from his father for "his investments in movie art."

He had a small apartment in suburbia, suitable for his activities. He inherited the space from his grandma, and he used it to make a movie studio. His task was to find pretty girls who would play the role of women slaves in his movie Masterpieces.

His expenses were enormous, without significant results. His porno movies had a few views and clicks, and comments from visitors were "boring," "ordinary," and "my grandma is sexier than your actors."

After Andrej lost his money, he called Denis to help him with his business. He did not want to give up. His childhood friend laughed at his idea at first, but later he accepted to become his partner.

"I know many women, and some of them are ready to drink urine for money. Just, you need something special. People are asking for more than pussy and dick nowadays. They want violence, pain, fetish. They want it to look real."

Denis researched and bought suitable equipment. He offered money in advance to women who wanted to have a career in acting. They knew they had to be naked and make love, but they accepted if their identity was hidden. So, their professional names became Sweet Patricia and Sexy Laura. They made a sexy duo.

For Andrej's upcoming scenario, they needed an innocent girl, someone who didn't know how she got there so it had an actual effect on the audience. Sweet Patricia and Sexy Laura would use the innocent girl as a slave. They would use her as a sexual toy, and the audience would enjoy every second.

Two male actors were present for the scenario, Gabrijel, and Ivan. Their role was to kidnap the victim and chain her down, like a slave. Only one thing was missing. Where would they find an elegant and decent girl, who was not in the porno industry and who would accept the role?

Denis went to social media and found Natalija's Instagram. They had a past together, and it reminded him what had happened on the beach. He could not resist her photos in her swimsuit.

Like many women nowadays, she wanted to be noticed to earn money from social media. She was working as a designer in a factory, but the job was far from her dreams. She wanted to sell her clothes around the world, work in the fashion industry and be the next Prada.

His plan was an entrance to hell. After he got involved with Maja, he realized luck was on his side because Natalija was dating Bruno, Maja's brother. Denis intentionally chose the Island of Pag as the place for their holiday. He wanted the approach to Natalija again.

.....

Maja was packing her things. She did not want to stay with Denis in the hotel anymore, even for a moment. She notified Bruno what had happened, and he helped her find a free apartment in Gajac, a small place on the Island of Pag. It was near Bruno's apartment, in case she might need him.

After Denis left for a swim in the morning, Maja used his absence to leave without explanation. She locked the doors, left the key under the doormat, and sent him a text to pick up his keys when he returned from the beach.

Meanwhile, Bruno sat with a coffee, on the terrace with Natalija. They were constantly arguing, and it was hard to find a balance between their attitudes.

"You should go to the police, my dear. My sister found your photos in Denis's phone, and you should get a restraining order against him for stalking you."

"Your sister was not kind to me. She dumped a drink on me at the club because she was jealous. Besides, I have no interest in him. If I go to the police, I must justify why I did not report him ten years ago. It will cause trouble for me."

"Just stay away from him. I saw he kissed you. Are you cheating on me with this prick, Natalija?"

"Now you are worried for your ego, not for me. Are you following me?"

"I wish you would be more careful. I was thinking we could leave this place. We can go to the Island Krk."

"No, I don't want to. I can handle this. Thanks for your help, but this is my problem. You better talk to your sister. If she attacks me again, it will not end well."

Natalija was stubborn as usual. She did not like Bruno's protective behavior toward Maja; he did not take Natalija's side when she needed it. In her conflict with his sister, Natalija was always losing.

She felt like she had a rival, but it was even worse. Brotherly love and commitment were more important for Bruno than his girlfriend.

She took a sip from her cup and grabbed her phone. The notification light was blinking. It was a message from Denis. "Hey, Natalija. What would you say about going with me on a small boat trip? Today is very nice weather."

Bruno frowned. "Who is that?"

"My mother. She is asking how I feel today. You know she is overreacting." Natalija lied again. At least someone was giving her attention and understood how she felt.

She replied to Denis's message: "Let's meet on the coast in a half-hour."

Chapter 7

The boat trip

It was a perfect day for sailing. The sun was up and reflected on the calm blue sea. Seagulls flew above and hovered at the sea's surface to catch fish. Natalija took a photo with her phone. She adored those birds. From afar, she saw a motorboat arriving near the coast, so she stepped closer to the board.

Denis approached her with a smile. He helped her climb and offered her a seat near the deck.

"This is the best view." He took a rope to untie the boat and turned the engine on again.

Natalija's hair flew in the wind. She was speaking loudly because the engine was noisy. "Where are we going? I must be back in one hour."

"Don't worry, you will be back on time. I wanted to show you the island. This view you can't have my car or by foot."

Denis was right. The view was fantastic. Big rocks surrounded by the deep sea were untouchable, and boats were sailing around. Passengers were taking photos while the wind was slow and refreshing. Natalija closed her eyes. She felt like she was in paradise.

With her doubts gone, she enjoyed the view. What could go wrong on such a beautiful day? She must stop thinking about the past. It was a mistake from her youth, and Denis had shown his regret.

Denis took out his phone and walked on the deck. Natalija heard only part of his conversation since the sounds of the boat engine and seagulls mixed with his spoken words.

"Yes, we are arriving. No need. Just a few drinks."

Natalija looked at him curiously. She did not expect to visit anyone. She stirred in her chair.

"We are going to Novalja. I must check out my engine there. I called the marine surveyor."

"Do you think something is wrong with the boat?"

"No, this is just a regular check. I do it every time I come here because if there are any technical errors, I will pay a penalty."

"I understand. I hope it will not last too long. I have a throbbing headache." Natalija looked at him with a grumpy expression.

She questioned herself if her decision to go on the boat with Denis was right. She often acted upon her mood, and her half-cocked character had already cost her.

"Just relax. Do you want a drink? I have excellent wine here."

"Sure. Just don't pour me too much."

Denis walked across the deck and returned with two glasses, each half-filled with a dark liquid.

"It is Cabernet Sauvignon. It will remove your seasickness. Don't worry, it happens if you are not used to sailing." Denis offered her glass in a friendly manner, and she drank it to the bottom. Within a few moments, she felt very tired, and her body collapsed in Denis's arms.

....

"Let's toast." Andrej's mouth extended into a wide smile when he finished his call. He sat on the beach with Gabrijel and Ivan, who looked at Natalija's photos. He had given them printed copies, to introduce his future star to the guys.

"Wow. This will be a sweet fuck. This peach will get a big banana." Gabrijel licked his lips, while Ivan smiled.

"I must correct you. This peach will get two big bananas."

They shook hands like they had finished an important business deal.

"Just do your best, guys. You know what our primary is: to enter the top ten of Gonzo," Andrej said in a bossy tone. "We are professionals, and we must act like it."

...

Bruno looked at his watch. "It's strange. Natalija should have been back in one hour."

Maja took his hand. "I told you, this girl is not trustful. I am sure she is seducing Denis again."

"When did you see him last?"

"In the morning. He took his motorboat keys and went out before I told him to fuck off forever."

"You said he has a motorboat?"

"Of course, this shit has a lot of money, but I had no use of it. He barely bought me a drink." Maja smirked.

"Where does he keep this boat? In the marine?"

"How should I know? I did not know he had something with your girlfriend, so do you think he is going to tell me about his business?"

"Just stop it, Maja. You are making me nervous. Can you at least recognize this boat?"

"You have luck there. I took a photo of it for my Instagram. Look, am I sexy?" Maja showed him a photo where she was in a short red skirt and high heels, and her hands were in the air like she could fly.

"Let's go to the police."

"Why? What will you tell them? That your girlfriend went on a trip with her new lover?"

Bruno was powerless. He kept calling Natalija, but nobody answered. The call was disconnected every time he tried.

"She would answer my call or send me a message. She is a responsible woman. Something happened. I feel it."

Chapter 8

Thalia's dream

The first thing Natalija noticed was an enormous bed. She was lying on it with spread legs, and she realized they had chained her arms with cuffs. To her horror, she was naked. She tried to scream, but in her mouth was a muzzle.

Then she noticed something else. She was not alone. In the corner was a tall, dark-haired man who held a camera, and its light was focused right on her.

"Excellent. Just put this Enigma song." Another man was making orders, and the music filled the room. She recognized it as the song "Mea Culpa" from Enigma.

Two men, who looked like they regularly trained in the gym, slowly approached her.

One started massaging her breasts, and the other fingered her slowly inside her crotch, moaning while he did it. They were on her like hungry animals.

Natalija watched through a mist. Her head hurt, and the room was spinning around. She wanted to move, but her legs were paralyzed. One man put his fist inside her vagina. She felt a sharp pain, like a knife penetrating through her.

"Zoom in," the man behind the camera said.

"It is dry. I need lube," a raspy voice answered. The man put a sticky fluid from a tube onto her and continued to push his fist inside.

"Stop it, Gabrijel. Enough. Now, the next scene."

The other man, who had curly hair and oiled muscles, moved on top of her. His penis was erect, and he came near her face.

"Your turn, Ivan," a deep voice ordered, and the man removed her muzzle. He opened her mouth with his fingers and pushed his penis inside. Natalija gagged, but the man held her jaw and pushed it farther.

She struggled to breathe, but his penis blocked her mouth. His fluid filled her throat, and she spat. His semen was all over her face, and the man laughed like an animal.

"This will be the top. Cut!" The deep voice sounded satisfied. "Now, let's take a lunch break. Give her water and wipe this cream. Nice work."

Two days later

Three guys were moving into the small room. There was weak light coming from a lamp and Denis sat near the computer, to see the scenes better.

"Now, this is a suitable material. She has a natural talent. How many clicks do we have?"

"We have thousand from yesterday. I called the video 'Thalia's dream.'" Andrej was proud of his idea. He smiled like he had won the lottery.

"I suggest we wait until tomorrow for part two, let our audience live in uncertainty, wondering what happens next. Now, we are getting somewhere."

"What are you planning to do next?" Andrej looked at Denis. He was the boss of the project, and Andrej trusted he would know what was best.

"Let it be ménage à trois. Gabrijel and Ivan will come together to fuck her at the same time."

"You think she can handle it?"

"I will send her Sexy Laura. She can give her advice. Let the girls talk."

...

A flood of humiliation overwhelmed Natalija. She was alone in the room, without handcuffs but tied with rope to the chair.

Someone had dressed her in her pants and a white T-shirt. The room had red curtains, and sun rays penetrated through it.

Suddenly, a woman in leather boots came into the room. She was a redhead and was dressed like a dominatrix. Her black leather bra was zipped in the front, and a short latex skirt exposed her long skinny legs.

"Hello, sweetheart. I am Laura." The woman sat near her and tapped her arm.

"Help me get out of here," Natalija said, trying to raise her voice. They gave her a lot of ice in her last glass of water, so she was speaking raspy, and every attempt to scream ended badly. She sounded like a crow.

"Sweetie. You will get used to it. I have been working in this industry for a year. You are the star now. I heard some news."

Natalija was terrified. "What are these guys doing to me?"

"Your video is called 'Thalia's dream.' You have over a thousand views on Gonzo, and people love you."

Tears were falling down Natalija's face.

"Oh, don't worry, dear. You must be focused on part two. They are coming today to make a new video."

"You must untie me. Please, set me free. I will pay you later. I am a fashion designer, and I can pay you. Just tell me your price."

"Honey, you work for us now. Forget your previous life. Listen to me, I know Gabrijel and Ivan have big toys." Laura chuckled. "But just use a lot of lube and tell them to slow down. Don't forget to smile. The audience loves it. You must look like you're in ecstasy."

"Please, I can't do it," Natalija begged her.

"You have until tomorrow to prepare, my dear. You can practice with a banana. It helps. I will bring you a cocktail and magic powder to relax. After you get used to it, you will ask for more." Laura winked and left the room.

....

Bruno sat on a bench at the police station. He had waited for an hour in front of the office, to report Natalija missing. Finally, a fat woman invited him inside.

"So, you say your fiancée left two days ago and has not called you?" The fat woman in a police uniform looked at him, writing something on the paper in front of her.

"Yes. It is not like her at all. She would always call," Bruno said in a sad tone. Guilt weighed on him; he felt responsible.

"Why did she leave? Were you arguing?"

"She and my sister cannot stand each other, but she said she would come back soon, and now there is no trace of her."

"Do you have any idea where she would go?"

Bruno felt like he was wasting time. He showed her his phone with the photo of the boat with Maja.

"I will call my people to search his apartment first. Then we will go to the marine. The boat must be near the coast."

"Can you call me if you find anything? Can I go with you?" Bruno begged.

"No, stay here, young man. What did you say was the name of the guy you suspect?"

"Denis Milić. He is thirty years old, and he is a violent guy."

"You suppose he is violent, or do you have proof? I will search for him in the database. Maybe he has a criminal record. Just wait for our call, do nothing stupid."

Chapter 9

The gathering

The morning breeze had a refreshing impact on Denis. He went to the liquor store to buy booze. While he was waiting in line, he saw the morning newspaper. On the front page was Natalija's photo and the title: A Young Tourist Disappeared on the Island of Pag."

He felt his skin crawl. He was not afraid of the police after he'd not been caught for raping her ten years ago. What he did not want was to fail with his plans. One mistake would cost him, and he was on the edge. He could get rich or caught, depending on what he did next.

"We will record part two today and then we must leave this island. I don't know what to do with Natalija." His thoughts were racing. He doubted Natalija could be of any use after they finished with her. "I should eliminate her so she doesn't become a threat."

Denis was violent and egocentric. It was not strange for him to rape or hit women if he felt it was necessary. Murder was something else. He had been clean of those dark thoughts until now.

Natalija's condition was not well, and if they released her, she could report them for abuse and pornography, also for kidnapping. He could spend the rest of his life in jail.

Maybe they could leave her on some island with a few inhabitants, without internet and television, but where would he find such a place? After he finished his project, he would be rich and could repay the loan from his father.

"Hey, young man, can you move?" The old lady interrupted the direction of his thoughts. It was his turn. He nodded and asked for a beer.

....

"You are a pussy. Also, you are a coward. Shall I call your mom?" The sound of mocking voices echoed in Bruno's ears. He sat near the beach and remembered how he could never stand up for himself, even to protect the people he loved.

When he was a kid, an older guy hit him in the head with a ball on a football field. Football was a favored sport in Croatia. He cried, and the other guys laughed at him. Soon after, they continued pranking him.

He used to sit on the bench at the field to watch other guys playing football. They set him up by putting a cockroach on the paper where he sat. He screamed, and the guys laughed.

When he grew up, he was an excellent student and a decent guy. He was also handsome, and every mother wanted him for a son-in-law. Girls who liked tough guys did not notice him. Some joked that he should go shopping with them.

He met Natalija in a student's restaurant. That blonde girl with big blue eyes immediately got his attention. She was struggling to cut a piece of meat with a knife.

"Excuse me, can I sit here? There are no seats at the other tables," he said, and she accepted.

The history of their relationship played like a movie in his mind. First date. First kiss. First time making love. Bruno always had a feeling that Natalija hid a dark secret. She was nervous, explosive, and depressive. Bruno thought she was a spoiled princess, but now he realized how many wrong conclusions he'd had about her.

A deep regret ate at him. He supported Maja because he had lost his parents in an accident many years ago. He had a duty to take care of her because she was a young and wild girl. During his commitment, he forgot he had a fiancée who needed his attention.

Many times, Natalija would tell him, "You have no guts," or, "You are a cuckold." It was true, because he jumped on Maja's every wish, and when she confronted Natalija, he did not defend his girlfriend.

He called his sister. "Listen, Maja, can you remember anything about Denis? What makes him suspicious?"

"Police searched the apartment. They did not find a thing. How can I help?"

"Look at his social media. You have a nose for this. Maybe you can remember something, his friends or relatives, to locate him. I can't wait anymore."

"You are not going alone, bro. I am finishing my shopping. Wait for me on the beach. I have an idea."

.....

Denis was grumpy. He was not in a good mood, and it was visible. He was a leader, and he gathered his team in the dining room to notify them about his plan.

"The police are searching for Natalija. We must rush with the movie. Do it within a few hours and then pack your things. We must get out of here."

Gabrijel raised his hand.

"I don't think the woman is ready. She is crying every time I see her. How we can record like that?"

"Shut up. Did I ask you for your opinion?" Denis raised his voice. "Use your charm. Make a sandwich and bring it to her. Be friendly and make her relax. You have one hour to get her ready."

Gabrijel frowned. He could not stand his boss, but Denis had given him money in advance, so Gabrijel swallowed his rage. If circumstances were different, he would shoot him.

"I must get out of here." Natalija's thoughts mixed with her paranoid mood, causing her to panic. "If that guy rapes me again, I will die. I will kill myself, so it is better to get out before it is too late."

The door of her room opened, and Gabrijel walked with a sandwich. It was the same guy who had fisted her. Natalija's first thought was to spit on him, but she changed her mind. Maybe it was the opportunity she was waiting for.

"Thank you. I can't eat with tied hands, so you will have to feed me." She did her best to show kindness and forced herself to smile.

"It is not a problem, honey. We'll have action in an hour. Let's plan about how we will manage it."

Natalija closed her eyes. So it was happening again. She must deal with it now.

"Why are you working here? You are a handsome man. You can earn money another way. This is a criminal act."

Gabrijel took a piece of bread and put it in her mouth. "Eat. You will need your strength. I prefer to come from the back. My penis is big, so it will probably hurt you. I'll spit on your ass to help my penis slide in. Ask Laura, we trained her too. She asked for more later."

Natalija pretended she did not hear him. "Can you set me free? I will give you head if you untie me. This is my final offer. Just help me."

Gabrijel thought about it. He liked stubborn and brave women. This blonde was both.

"It is a tempting offer, but—"

"Tell them the knot was not well tied. And I escaped when you were on the toilet."

Gabrijel unzipped his pants. He grabbed Natalija's hair with one hand and pulled her close.

"Do it."

Natalija did not have a choice. She put his penis in her mouth and sucked it.

"Wow... Oh... good girl... good girl..." Gabrijel repeated himself until he spilled his fluid inside her mouth. She spat it out.

Natalija took a sip of water from the glass near her. "Hurry."

Gabrijel untied the knot. It was more intricate than he'd thought, so he looked for scissors. After a few minutes, he found a pair and cut the rope.

"Get out by the back door. This house has a courtyard, and they open the fence daily. Just go left and downstairs. They are all in the dining room now, preparing for a session."

Gabrijel gave her a pair of sneakers. "Laura left them here. They will fit you. Now, run!"

Chapter 10

The escape

"Are we ready, guys?" Denis glared at his team. "Ivan, you are going first, then Gabrijel is after you. Sandi, you are responsible for the sound. Find something mystical, like Gregorians. Frane, you will use the HD camera. Laura, make her a cocktail; she will need it. Andrej, do we have a fast internet connection? I want it uploaded immediately when it finishes. I must do this in one hour and then we are leaving."

The group climbed the stairs. Laura opened the door and found Gabrijel alone. He was drinking his beer, and his legs were on the armchair, cowboy style.

"Where is Natalija?" Denis yelled.

"I do not understand. She said she would shit her pants, so I let her go to the toilet."

"You are a fucking moron. What did I tell you? To take care of her!"

"What was I supposed to do, let her poop here?" Gabrijel smiled. He looked like he was having fun.

Denis took Gabrijel's bottle and spilled his beer on the floor.

"Idiot. We have police at our backs. Andrej, she could not go far. Take your motorbike, and I will go on foot. If you see her, call me immediately. I will catch the bimbo, and she will pay for this."

....

The yellow bus stood at the station, and Bruno took his seat. Maja followed him and said, "Denis mentioned friends in Novalja. We should go to the bar called Cocomo there. It is a popular place. But I left the jerk, so I can visit it alone."

"We have no time for a party now. Did you bring the posters?"

"Yes, here they are. There are probably plenty of notices about her missing in the city, but just in case, I have more." Maja looked at the posters with Natalija's photo and the words: Missing Person.

She almost felt sorry for his brother, but her intolerance toward Natalija was still in the air. She did not like Natalija, and she could not change her opinion overnight.

"Good. Do you know his friends? Are they in the house or the apartment?"

"How should I know? Novalja is a party destination, so they could have rented anything there. If they are idiots like Denis, I suppose they would choose a house to take whores to."

....

Natalija heard footsteps near her. She saw a pair of Denis's shoes while she hid in the bush, trying not to move. She moved to near the neighbor's house because Denis was so close and he was sneaking around like a hunter.

It was a vast garden. The house was probably owned by rich people who vacationed there. Luckily, there was no dog; otherwise, she would be noticed immediately.

"Where are you, filthy whore?" Denis yelled. He looked left and right. A cat ran in front of him, startled. After Denis did not find his target, he moved out of Natalija's sight.

Natalija held her breath. It had been too close. She was without money or a phone, and the sneakers she wore were uncomfortable. Her face was dirty, and she had bruises on her arms. She went to the bus station. She could enter the crowd there and try to not pay for a ticket, or she could ask someone for coins.

She went to the seafront where there was an enormous crowd. The bus station was near, and young people stood in line to travel to the afternoon party on Zrće Beach.

"Excuse me." Natalija tapped the shoulder of a guy with an earring. "Do you have some coins? I lost my wallet, and I need to go home."

The guy looked at her with pity and gave her a few coins. "You look pretty bad, babe. Someone hit you?"

"Yes, but it doesn't matter. I just want to go home." Natalija thanked him and sat in her place.

Denis noticed the crowd at the bus station and approached. There were three buses ready for departure. He pushed people around and showed them Natalija's photo.

"Have you seen this chick? She is my girlfriend. I need to find her," he pleaded. Nobody told him they had, so he peered at bus windows and finally noticed Natalija sitting toward the back of one. When he tried to enter the bus, the driver started the engine, and the door closed.

"Wait! I need to get on."

"Sorry, dude. The bus is full. Wait for the next one." The older driver waved him off.

Denis swore. "When the next bus is coming?" he asked around.

"They drive by every half hour," a girl nearby answered him, looking at his muscles curiously.

Denis pulled out his phone. "Hello, Andrej. The bitch is on the bus toward Zrće Beach. Go there with your motorbike and ambush her. The bus stand near the forest. She should come in that direction. I will be there in half an hour."

...

While the bus was going down the road, Natalija looked at the posters they passed. There were announcing big party events at the clubs. She was supposed to have been there, according to her plans, but who would have expected what had happened on this vacation?

She was traumatized, but she did not have time to think about it. Her survival instinct was stronger than her shame or guilt. She had a plan. After she cleaned herself in the sea, she would walk to her apartment. Then Bruno could call the police.

She knew Denis was hunting her, but she had an advantage. The beach was full of young people. Afternoon parties didn't start until four in the afternoon. If Denis tried to catch her, he wouldn't be able to do anything in the public place. Security was everywhere, and he would not play the bad guy.

The bus arrived at its destination. The forest came up to the beautiful, big beach, and Velebit Mountain offered a beautiful view.

The Island of Pag was famous with legend, with a story about people claiming that aliens had visited the island.

However, a tourist came every year to see it and to listen to electronic music at party festivals.

....

"Nothing. Nobody saw her." Bruno let out a sigh. "Maybe the bastard killed her."

"You have a wild imagination, bro. Denis is a prick, but he cannot kill anyone. I know he wouldn't." Maja smirked.

"I will call the police detective to find out if there is new info about Natalija."

"There is nothing you can do. Now, I suggest you go to Zrće Beach because there is an afternoon party. It is better to be outside than to wait at home in this heat," Maja told him.

It was a hot day. The temperature was climbing to over thirty-five Celsius, and Maja wiped the sweat from her face.

"Please. I need to go to the beach."

…

Natalija wanted to swim, but she had no swimsuit. If she swam in the shirt, it would get wet and she would get cold. Besides, she would bring attention to herself. She could not swim topless either. Some maniac could be always around, and she was alone.

She waited for the perfect opportunity. While a guy was bungee-jumping, the crowd of his friends watched him. They shattered their things on the beach, and girls were clapping their hands and screaming, rooting for their friend.

One girl was changing clothes and put her bra on top of the cabin next to her. Natalija grabbed it immediately and ran into the forest to put it on. While she was running, she slipped on a branch and fell.

"So, here you are, sleeping beauty," a familiar voice said near her ears. Andrej was smiling and grabbed her by the hair.

"Let me go."

"You are going with me. We have some unfinished business. Remember, you are a porno star."

Natalija was desperate. She struggled to get out of his embrace, but his grip was too tight.

"What is going on here?" Bruno appeared in front of them, holding a rock.

Andrej laughed. "Oh, here is your beloved fiancé. Your Prince Charming. What will you do to me?"

"Let her go. It is easy to attack an innocent woman. Try me."

"Innocent? She is as innocent as a Madam from a brothel. Ask her about her porno star career. Or better, watch Gonzo tonight. Her movie is near the top ten. Do you like fisting or swallowing?"

Bruno threw the rock toward him, but it missed the target. Andrej dragged Natalija deeper into the forest. All around were empty bottles, trash left behind from parties. Drunk teenagers would stash their booze under the trees and then drink it in the morning after they woke with a hangover.

If someone were not careful enough, they could get cut on the broken glasses.

Suddenly, Andrej felt a powerful blow to his head and collapsed on the ground.

Blood flowed from his brow, and Bruno looked at Andrej with disbelief. His glare then focused at Maja, who appeared from behind a tree.

Maja stood above Andrej and held what remained of a big empty bottle in her hands. It was smashed in half, and shattered pieces of glass had fallen to the grass. Andrej's head was bleeding, but she did not care.

She said in a nervous tone, "Let's get out of here before he gets up."

"Thank you," Natalija whispered in shock. "But where is Denis?"

There was no sign of Denis in the forest. Bruno called the emergency line, looking at Andrej who lay on the ground, blood dripping down his face.

"He doesn't deserve to live." Bruno frowned. "But I don't want to be responsible for his miserable life."

Chapter 11

24 hours later

After the police officer finished their report, he told Bruno, Maja, and Natalija to give their statements. Natalija confirmed the abuse and kidnapping, Maja said she intentionally injured Andrej to help Natalija, and Bruno confirmed about calling the emergency line.

"We arrested four guys and two girls in Novalja. They are being detained now," the police officer told them. "The guy you talked about, Denis Milić, escaped. You must stay local in case we have more questions, so don't leave this island until I say you can."

Bruno was not happy with this news. He wanted to go back to their city as soon as possible, but he nodded anyway.

"We have enough to file an indictment, but we need you as witnesses. The guy who got a blow to the head is in the hospital and said he will collaborate with us."

"I knew Andrej was a real snitch," Natalija murmured.

"For your protection, we will send a patrol car to sit in front of your apartment. You can feel safe."

Bruno and Natalija agreed to this, because Denis was still somewhere, so the danger had not vanished.

....

Denis had been a scout in his youth. He learned how to manage in the forest, how to cover himself with leaves, and how to reorient himself. Also, he was not devoted to anyone.

His friends had been arrested, but it did not bother him. He played the role of a homeless person. Nobody paid attention to a guy in rags, and his kind was not rare here.

He drank beer and whiskey from bottles he found in the woods. Thanks to the party zone, the liquor was available. Party people left it in the bushes, in plastic bags, and on the ground because some of them were sleeping in the forest or on the beach. Their lips were always dry from drugs so they needed backup with alcohol.

Denis knew it was dangerous to come back to the house, but the keys to his boat and everything he needed to leave this area were there. The police had picked up his equipment, and Andrej would for sure betray him, but he needed to survive this week and then he could try to leave the island. He had no money. His bank cards were empty because of his expenses, which was another problem.

Despite all his troubles, Denis still had an itch to catch Natalija. It was almost his mission. He felt something was not finished, and if he caught her, she could be his hostage and his ticket for escape.

He saw a patrol car in front of their apartment, but he already had a plan. That police officer was probably as hungry as every police officer. He would order some food, and Denis would pretend he was the delivery boy—after he got rid of the real one.

He was sneaking around the street near the apartment, and when he saw the bike he'd been waiting for, he jumped out of the bush in front of the guy.

"Hey, pal. Do you have some money?"

"No, I don't. Get out from my way."

"As you wish," Denis said and smashed him in the nose. Before the guy came, Denis picked up the bike and rode until he got to the apartment. He waved at the police officer to get out of the car and pick up the food.

"Any tips?" he asked the police officer when he accepted the paper bag.

The policeman was searching his wallet, but Denis grabbed a discarded bottle he found lying on the ground, probably left by party people as they passed the apartments, and smashed it against the man's head. Then he jumped the fence and entered the apartment, where Natalija slept with an open window. It was on the ground floor.

Denis sneaked through the darkroom and saw only Bruno, who slept peacefully in his bed. He heard the sound of water from the bathroom. Natalija was in there, having problems with her sleep.

She was washing her face, trying to calm down. She had woken up from a nightmare where she saw someone was taking her away, but she did not know who it was.

She heard a weird sound like someone is tapping on the door. Instinctively, she grabbed a razor. It was near the mirror, and the first thing she thought about was how it could be a useful weapon. Bruno had left the razor when he finished his usual shaving yesterday.

Denis opened the door with a creaking sound.

He showed her a smashed bottle and held it toward her, like a weapon.

"Leave with me and nothing bad will happen."

"Please leave me alone," Natalija replied in shock, squeezing the razor in the pocket of her bathrobe.

"Leave with me or I will hurt your boyfriend."

Natalija thought quickly. This had to be finished, once and for all. She was not afraid anymore. Her wish to get out of the situation was stronger than her fear.

"Okay. This is between you and me. Let's go out and talk," she said, trying to sound calm.

Bruno was sleeping like nothing was happening. Natalija and Denis sneaked out of the room and went to the beach.

It was about three in the morning and the beach was empty. Moonlight reflected off the sea, the only source of light.

"Ready for a night swim with me?" Denis smirked.

"You are so egocentric. Why should I listen to you?"

"Come on. You liked it when I fucked you. You were insatiable. You enjoyed when my guys fucked you in your mouth. You are a whore. Gabrijel said you gave him head. And your movie... Babe, you will make me a lot of money."

He was approaching her, while she stepped back toward the sea. His words echoed in her ears.

"Let's deal, babe. You and I can earn a fortune. I will be your pimp, and you will use your talent. It's a shame you did not do the ménage à trois movie with Gabrijel and Ivan. You would have enjoyed yourself."

"Don't you want to kiss me?" Natalija suddenly smiled. Her eyes shined under the moonlight.

"I will fuck you right now," Denis smirked. "You are my porno star."

"Come to me and give me pleasure." Natalija approached him, staying half in the seawater, the waves splashing her knees.

Her bathrobe was wet against her body, her nipples visible through the material. Denis felt lust and wanted to have her immediately.

Denis stepped closer to touch her face. "You are my whore."

Natalija let him embrace her. While his hands pulled her to his chest, she took the razor from her pocket and cut his neck. Blood streamed into the sea. Denis staggered and slipped on a rock. Natalija kneeled and repeated the cut a few times on autopilot. His eyes bulged. He was struggling to breathe.

He murmured words on his last sigh, "You damn fucking whore."

Natalija stood and calmly watched his body float along the sea's surface under the silver moonlight. Blood mixed with the saltwater, leaving Denis's body. Small fishes were swimming around his corpse-like numb witnesses.

Natalija threw the razor on the beach and started to wash her hands. Somewhere from afar, she heard police sirens.

Chapter 12

One year later

Dolus repentinus is a Latin phrase for the direct intent caused by sudden stimuli. It was a familiar term in Swiss criminal law, as a state of long-lasting pain, and was used for cases in domestic violence, when a wife killed her husband after many years of abuse.

Natalija had been accused of committing a criminal act against body and life, murder according to Croatian criminal law. Denis's parents hired the most expensive lawyer to prove her guilt. They wanted a verdict of intended murder.

His lawyer based his accusation on Natalija's behavior, and they delivered her porno movie as proof of her immorality. Natalija confessed her act. She had some gaps in her memory of when she'd been in that house.

A team of psychiatrists sat on a panel and announced their report. Her diagnosis was a state of mental disorder, caused by paranoia and dolus repentinus.

She described her act as if it were a mission of justice. "He was playing with my life, so I took his. He made the sea dirty with his blood. His body was sleeping in the waves."

Maja witnessed in her defense, making Natalija appear to be a caring person. Gabrijel negotiated with Natalija's lawyers. He witnessed in her defense and described Natalija as a victim. He winked at her after their eyes met in the courtroom. After Natalija's lawyers found out about the rape situation ten years ago, which had not been reported, they invited Luka to be a witness.

He described Denis with these words: "I was wondering when the day would come when he'd have to pay for his acts. He did not care about anyone; he played with people like they were toys."

Natalija got a verdict. She had been found guilty of manslaughter with diminished responsibility. The court took all circumstances, her previous raping, kidnapping, the forced porno movie, and Denis's behavior toward her.

Her punishment was two years in prison with an obligated psychiatric treatment. She could be released after one year, based on her behavior. The prison board, comprised of six members, was deciding about her release today.

Also, Natalija's lawyer pressed charges against Andrej and the rest of the team, for kidnapping and making a porno movie for distribution without her consent. After some problems, the movie was removed from porno sites, and the movie studio was closed and sealed.

Bruno waited for the news. Despite all that had happened, he loved Natalija. He felt guilty for not being man enough to protect her. He had visited her during the year to prove he cared about her. She was on her medical treatment, and often their conversation was short.

The court had accepted her request for early release after she spent one year in prison. The prison board was questioning terms for her release. Her behavior was on her side.

She was cleaning, spending time in the prison library, and being empathetic with the other prisoners. Women in the prison had heard about her porno movie and even provoked her, but Natalija never responded.

She smiled when they called her a porno star like she had some benefit from it. Her medical treatment offered improvement. She had no aggressive acts, and her health was good.

Bruno was sitting in a chair in the waiting room, looking at his phone. He wanted to make time move faster by playing the game. The guard, a woman with short hair, waved him to come near the protective glass, where prisoners were talking with their visitors.

Natalija approached the glass dressed in a denim suit, as it was the official outfit in Croatian prisons.

"How do you feel today?" Bruno asked, trying not to upset her. Natalija responded with a big smile. "They will release me tomorrow. I need to fill out some paperwork, and I will get a supervisor to monitor my behavior when I get out. They said I will be under a magnifier during my probation, whatever that means."

"That is glorious news, my dear. When do you want me to pick you up?"

"In the morning. I am a morning type, remember?"

Bruno smiled back. "I'll never forget."

After a long moment, Natalija's face shined. Her hair was dirty, and her face was drained, but nobody could deny her beauty, even in the ugly denim suit that every woman in the prison hated.

THE END

Read other books from Kristina Gallo:

Husband For Rent

Viktorija is a psychologist. She is working in an office-sponsored by Government and helps migrants with asylum applications. Her ex-husband Boris tries to maintain their connection after the divorce, and she wishes to be rid of him.

While on her lunch break, Viktorija meets Jamal, a waiter who is a migrant from Algeria, and befriends him. Jamal lives with his family in a rented flat in Croatia. His wife, Meriem, has health issues. She becomes jealous because of Jamal's affairs. Viktorija gets abusive emails, but she can't discover the sender. Soon someone from Viktorija's business circle is murdered. Viktorija will find out stunning facts about her colleagues, Nina and Tamara. What will the fight for survival cost her?

'A suspenseful thriller of contemporary situations in Europe. Reading it, you'll want more. You can tell that English isn't the writer's first language, but read through it. Her stories make you think of the human condition and consequences of one's actions. Written in a different mindset. Take a read and expand your horizons.' 5* Amazon Review.

The Player Without Luck

When Silvija found a dead body in the casino, it looked like an accident. Did it involve the work of hitman? A man who knew a dirty secret from her past blackmailed her. She had a motive for the murder because a ruined reputation could cause her to lose her job and husband. Her affair with a security guard, Ivan, will complicate things further. She wanted to be safe, but Ivan was involved deeper than she thought.

'Given that Ms Gallo has written this book in a language that is not her native one, her ability to weave such an impressive and twisted yarn is testament to her superb story-telling skills and command of a story that creates a continuous air of mystery and suspense within it. Highly recommended.' 5* Amazon Review.

Made in the USA
Monee, IL
20 July 2023

39645881R00072